Forest Babies

Stories by
JEAN J. PARRISH

Illustrations by
ELIZABETH WEBBE

RAND MᶜNALLY & COMPANY · Chicago

BUFFIN GOES EVERYWHERE

Hello, World!" said Buffin, running to the door of the hollow tree and looking out. The sun was shining down in spots, and Buffin was a new bear.

"Where are you off to?" his father said sleepily.

Buffin spread his little paws wide over his head and shouted, "Oh, everywhere!"

"Then I'd better go with you," said Father Bear, "and take you there, one place at a time."

But Buffin was off and away before Father Bear could tumble out of bed.

"I'll visit the ants," he said to himself.

The ants lived in a little red hill with a hole in the top, and they spent the whole day hustling and bustling.

Buffin sniffed at the anthill in a friendly way; then all at once he squealed and backed away. The busy ants had no time for nosey bears, and Buffin's nose was stung good and proper.

But a bear who is going everywhere has to go somewhere, so Buffin forgot the hurt and went on till he smelled honey in the air.

The nice smell was coming from a tall tree.

"Sniff, sniff, and up I go!" said Buffin to himself, and up he went. There, sure enough, was a hole in the tree, and honey smells coming out of it. Buffin put his nose in for a lick of honey, but the bees would not have such doings in their tree!

"*Ouch! Ouch!*" cried Buffin, climbing down backward as fast as he could. Just before he reached the bottom, he took a back somersault and landed WHOP! in the thickest cocklebur patch in the whole forest.

"A pretty how-de-do!" said Buffin, as he crawled out with the burs sticking to his fur. His nose was *really* hurting this time, and he held it with one paw while he ran on the other three straight to the little pond and rolled around in the cool mud—because all bears know that mud is good for stings.

"What strange animal is this coming up our path?" said Father Bear when he saw Buffin.

Mother Bear started picking out the burs and scraping off the mud and rubbing the stings with honey.

When the mud was out of his ears, they said, "Where *have* you been?"

"Everywhere," Buffin said in a little voice.

The next morning Buffin crawled out of bed, rubbed his nose, and said to his father, "Let's go honeying *together* today!"

And while his father was waking up and getting started, he heard Buffin say as cheerily as ever, "Hello, World!"

BUNNIFER TRIES IT OUT

BUNNIFER was all mixed up.

"When I learn to swim," he said to his mother, "I'll swim to the bottom of Rushing Brook and gather some nice green things for you." He made swimming motions with his feet.

"You weren't meant to swim, Bunnifer," said his mother. But Bunnifer didn't wait to hear the rest. He hopped down over the brown leaves to Rushing Brook and sat waiting.

Soon Little Frog came to the top and Bunnifer said, "Show me how to swim!"

Little Frog did a few long strokes under water.

Bunnifer saw how it was done and cried, "Hurray!" and tumbled into the water topsy-turvy. For a minute he didn't know what was happening to him. There was water over him and mud in his eyes and Little Frog was darting madly all around him. Then somehow or other Bunnifer scrambled onto the bank and hopped home, shivering with brook water.

"I suppose I'm really not the swimming sort of rabbit," said Bunnifer as he dried out in the sun.

A few days later, when he was sitting outside the burrow, he saw his friend, Tanager, fly over.

"When I learn to fly," Bunnifer said, "I'll go up and tell you what I see outside the forest." And he made flying motions with his paws.

"You weren't meant to fly," his mother said.

But Bunnifer was already headed for a fallen tree that slanted across the path. With jolly little jumps he went up to the highest end. And there was Tanager flying over.

Bunnifer said, "Whee!" and jumped into the air after Tanager. But he tumbled right down through the doorway of his own burrow.

"I suppose I'm really not the flying sort of rabbit," he said as he picked himself up.

"You weren't meant to swim and you weren't meant to fly," said his mother. "But you're the hoppety-hop sort of rabbit, and you can hoppety-hop and jumpety-jump better than *anybody*. Now just you hoppety-hop down to the swamp and get some of those nice greens for your supper!"

And off went Bunnifer, jumping high and wide. When he saw Tanager, he wiggled his tall ears at him and said, "I may not fly, but I can hoppety-hop!"

And when he passed Rushing Brook, he wiggled his tall ears at Little Frog and said, "I may not swim, but just look at me jumpety-jump!"

ROLY AND POLY GET DIZZY

THE raccoon twins looked so much alike that no one could tell which was which. Roly had a high forehead—but then, so did Poly! Poly had bright eyes—but then, so did Roly!

When the animals in the forest asked Roly how *he* could tell which was which, he just said, "Well, you see, Poly has a Poly look, and I haven't."

And when they asked Poly, he said, "It's very simple. Roly has a Roly look, and I haven't."

So Roly and Poly never got mixed up, but everyone else did.

On the slope of Rushing Brook there was an old hollow log where Roly and Poly went to play every day. Roly would hide very quietly, and when Poly found him they would roll around and pommel each other and giggle. Then it would be Poly's turn to hide.

Then they would chase each other into one
end of the old log and out of the other end. Once
their noise woke up Sleepy Owl in the oak tree.
He peered out and watched them for a long time.
Then he shook his head and said, "I never saw a
raccoon run so fast in all my life. Right while he's
going in one end, he's coming out the other!"

With that Roly and Poly stopped, and he saw that there were two of them.

"How do you know which is yourself, or don't you?" he said.

But Roly only looked at Poly and said, "He's the one with the Poly look."

As the twins grew older and stronger, they ran so fast through the hollow log that it fairly trembled and shook. One day they ran through it, round and round, a *hundred times*.

"A hundred and one," puffed Roly.

"A hundred and two," puffed Poly.

But on the "hundred and three" they both fell to the ground, as dizzy as May flies, and lay looking up at the sky.

"The clouds are whirling round and round," said Roly.

"The ground is going up and over," said Poly.

Then they heard their mother calling, and they got up and went plunging and tumbling along the bank of the brook toward home. When they passed the quiet pool, Roly stopped to look at himself. He was so dizzy he didn't know whether he was upside down or not!

"Is that you or I?" he said.

"It's you," said Poly who, by now, was not quite so dizzy.

"How can you tell?" said Roly.

"Because you have a Roly look," said Poly.

"That's all right then—as long as you're sure. It would be awful if *we* got mixed up about it!"

And they ran on home, tumbling over each other and giggling all the way.

LITTLE DEER GETS A NAME

WHEN Little Deer was only a few days old, he looked up at his mother and said, "Why can't I have a name all my own—like Buffin and Bunnifer? No one calls Buffin, 'Little Bear,' or Bunnifer, 'Little Rabbit'! Why must I always be called 'Little Deer'?"

"Well, you see, it's this way," answered his mother. "We deer have to earn our names. 'Flash' was named that because he can run so fast. 'Lightfoot' earned his name because his feet hardly touch the ground. And 'Long Antlers' grew the longest antlers."

Little Deer thought about this as he stumbled through the forest on his wobbly new legs.

"Then, if it's that way," he said out loud to himself, "I'll be named 'Clumsy' or 'Bumper' or 'Straddle-Bug.'"

"Why?" said Buffin, popping his head out from the hollow log.

"Just watch the way I jump, if you want to know," said Little Deer. "Watch!"

He wobbled up to the hollow log, gave a weak little jump, and landed right on top of it. Then he squirmed and wiggled over and fell on the other side, with his legs all ways.

"You can't jump because you think you can't," said Buffin, starting down the path to Rushing Brook.

"I think I can't because I *can't*," said Little Deer, picking himself up and following.

Down by the brook they found a bush covered with big ripe blackberries. It was very quiet in the

forest as they stood on the bank, munching the juicy berries. Not a breeze was stirring the trees, and the only sound was the rushing of the brook.

All of a sudden came the sharp snap of a twig. Little Deer was so startled that he sailed into the air like a bird and came down on the opposite bank.

Then he turned to see what had made the noise, and there stood his mother beside Buffin.

"How would you like to be called 'White-tailed Flier'?" she asked.

But Little Deer couldn't answer a word—because it was such a *beautiful* name.

SQUIFFY MAKES A RESCUE

SQUIFFY was a show-off. When he was a little baby, he began it. "Such a show-off," all the animals said.

"Watch me!" he said one day in the nest. His little sisters watched with wide eyes while he climbed up the side.

"Look!" he shouted. "Famous Flying Squirrel!" He jumped into the air and landed with a flop on his sisters. They said, "Ouch, my back!" and things like that. But Puff, the littlest one, said, "He *did* almost fly!"

That wasn't enough for Squiffy. The next day he said, "Stand back and look at the Great Twirler!" So they stood back and watched him jump up high and twirl around once before coming down. It was a handsome stunt, but he came down PLOP on the head of Mother Squirrel, who was just coming in the door.

"You looked nice up there, twirling," said Puff.

"Show-offs are bad," said Mother Squirrel, when her head was better. "Show-offs are silly. They say, 'Look at me' when there are silly things to do, but when there are *important* things to do, they just sit down and curl their tails around them."

That was a long speech for Mother Squirrel, and Squiffy thought about it in his bed that night.

The next day, although it was raining, Mother Squirrel went out to get pussy-willow buds for dinner. When she had been gone a long time, the

little squirrels suddenly noticed that Puff was no longer in the nest. They rushed to the door and looked down, and there, sitting in a cold puddle and weeping besides, was the littlest sister.

There was a great chatter in the nest. It was raining hard and the puddle was getting deeper and everything was dreadful.

Squiffy had never been to the ground before, but he put his back feet out over the edge and started backing down the tree. Halfway down he let go and dropped into the puddle with Puff.

Puff climbed onto his back and held on tight while Squiffy dug his nails in and climbed up the tree as far as the first branch. There he rested, and then he climbed to the second branch. He could hear his sisters crying and chattering above.

On the third try he reached the doorway and dumped Puff over the edge into the nest.

When Mother Squirrel came home and saw
Puff all wet and shivering, she said, "Squiffy, what
have you been up to?" But Squiffy just sat
down and curled his tail around him.

Then his little sisters said, "He did a *very
important thing!* And this time he didn't say
'Watch me!'—not once!"